Worry Warriors is published by Stone Arch Books,
A Capstone Imprint
1710 Roe Crest Drive
North Mankato, Minnesota 56003
www.mycapstone.com

Library of Congress Cataloging-in-Publication Data on file with Library of Congress,
available on their website.

ISBN 978-1-4965-3611-2 (library binding)
ISBN 978-1-4965-3650-1 (paperback)
ISBN 978-1-4965-3654-9 (ebook pdf)

Summary: Adam is excited to be on the soccer team, but he's nervous about taking
the five-paragraph essay test. If he flunks, he'll have to go back to tutoring. That
would mean the end of soccer for the year.

Editor: Michelle Bisson
Designer: Hilary Wacholz

Printed in Canada.
009643F16

Anxious Adam
Braves the Test

by Marne Ventura
illustrated by Leo Trinidad

STONE ARCH BOOKS
a capstone imprint

TABLE OF CONTENTS

ALL ABOUT THE
Worry WARRIORS

My name is Adam Brown. I live with my family in a city near the beach in California. I'm nine years old. Mom says I got my red hair, freckles, and green eyes from my dad. He died in a car accident before I was born. Another thing I have in common with my dad is dyslexia. That means I learn to read and write differently from most people. My favorite things are sports, art, and building projects. When I grow up I want to be an architect, artist, or soccer player. My three absolute best friends ever live on my block. We've been friends since preschool. We work together to help one another out.

Estella is an expert on movies and TV shows. She knows the names of all the actors, especially the kids. She loves dancing and cheerleading. She also likes hanging out with her faimly.

Jake loves to read, like I do. He's good at math, science, and computers. He wants to be a scientist someday. He's saving up for a robot race car.

Nellie likes reading, writing, word games, and school. That's excellent because she wants to be a writer when she grows up.

Three summers ago when we were six, we were making hula hoop bubbles in Nellie's backyard. We were barefoot, running around on the wet grass. Estella almost stepped on a bee. She freaked out, ran onto Nellie's back porch, and wouldn't budge until I scooped up the bee with a plastic cup and put it into the trashcan.

Then Estella said she felt silly, being scared of teeny bees. But she also said she felt better after she told us and we didn't laugh at her.

I guess Nellie didn't want Estella to feel silly alone, because she told us that she was afraid of the dark at bedtime. She imagined scary stuff, like that her toys might come to life and attack her, or that coyotes might be hiding in her closet.

Then Jake said he was afraid to wade into the ocean because he could feel slimy stuff with his feet. Plus, what if he stepped on a poison jellyfish?

So I told my friends my own babyish secret. I got scared walking across the bridge over the freeway. I held on tight to my mom's hand and didn't look down.

After we told each other our worries, we felt better. We didn't make fun of each other, like some kids would. And, we realized, if all of us had secret worries, maybe they weren't silly at all.

That's when Nellie had a great idea. She said we should form a club. First we would tell each other our worries. Then together we would fight them, like knights and warrior princesses in shining armor.

And that's how we became the Worry Warriors.

Chapter 1

Essay Test

It's a Tuesday morning in February. I'm at my desk in Ms. Anderson's fourth grade class. Estella sits in front of me. She's leaning forward, writing answers to multiplication problems. I finished mine, so I'm drawing in my sketchbook. I use long pencil strokes to show Estella's long hair.

While I draw, I think about soccer. The first practice of the season is today after school. I wonder who the coach will be? Who else will be on the team? I wish it were time to go right now. I draw a soccer ball. I add curved lines above and below, so it looks like it's flying across the field.

"Estella, will you please collect the math papers?" Ms. Anderson walks to the whiteboard. "Time to work on our five-paragraph essays." I groan as I hand Estella my worksheet and pull my language arts notebook out of my desk.

"Again?" Jake's seat is to my left. He hands Estella his page. "Seems like we're good on essay-writing."

"Maybe *you're* good." Estella adds Jake's paper to the stack. "I don't think I'm ever going to get it."

I feel the same way as Estella. We've been learning to write essays since the beginning of the school year, and I still get mixed up. Each of the paragraphs has to do a special job. In the right order. Spelling counts. I draw a quick sketch of Spelling, my evil anti-hero. He wears a black suit with a backwards S on his chest. He has an ugly face. Good thing I have a secret weapon—the spell checker on my computer.

"Let's review." Ms. Anderson writes ESSAY on the whiteboard. "Who can tell me what goes into each paragraph? Jake?"

Jake pushes his glasses up on his nose. "Introduction, three supporting paragraphs, and conclusion."

"Good." Ms. Anderson nods. "So far, we've been working together to outline our essays. Today, you're going to write your own outline."

Estella hands me a paper.

Ms. Anderson writes NARRATIVE, EXPOSITORY, and PERSUASIVE on the board. "Listen up, class. Let's review. Adam, please remind us what narrative means."

Luckily, I know this. "It's like a story," I say. "Something you did. An experience."

"Nice job," says Ms. Anderson. "How about expository—Estella?"

"Um, it's to convince someone to do something?" Estella swings her feet under her desk.

"That's persuasive. Try again?" Ms. Anderson smiles at Estella.

"Oh," she tries. "Expository is when you give information about something."

"Good job." Ms. Anderson turns to Riley. "Will you please read the topic, Riley?"

I follow along as Riley reads. *If you could pick any animal for class pet, what would you choose and why?* Oh, no. I've never had a pet. Mom's allergic.

"In this essay," Ms. Anderson continues, "you're going to give information about why an animal makes a good pet. Ryan, will this essay be narrative, expository, or persuasive?"

Ryan scratches his head. "Umm … expository?"

"Right," she says. "Because the purpose is to give the reader information."

I sigh and draw a gorilla in my sketchbook. I just watched a cool show about mountain gorillas in Africa. I could write about that. But if Ms. Anderson keeps talking, I won't have time. I was hoping for no homework tonight, since I have soccer practice.

"An essay about the day your pet hamster escaped is …?" Ms. Anderson asks. Most of us yell out *"Narrative,"* though a few people start to say *"Expository."* Ms. Anderson smiles and writes NARRATIVE on the board. "An essay that explains why hamsters make good pets is …?"

Estella says shyly, *"Expository,"* and Ms. Anderson says, "Good job. And ... an essay that tries to convince me to get a hamster as a pet is ... ?" We all yell out, "Persuasive!" We know that's the only one left.

Any questions?" Ms. Anderson says. We all shake our heads *no* even if we're not certain.

I look up at the chart that shows the steps for essay writing. Then I write *IDEEAS* across the top of my scratch paper. Next I write down words. *Gorilas—playful—eat plans and insets—smrat.* Wow, I already have three reasons why a gorilla makes a good pet.

I start in on the first reason.

1. rogilla is a good classroom pet cuz it's plaful.

Now what? I know I need more than one sentence. I open my language-arts notebook. Oh, right. I need three examples about gorillas being playful.

1. Gorillas lik to swing from trees, so kibs cood play with them on the plaaground at recess.

2. Young gorillas like to restle and guf around, just like kidz.

3. Rogillas ar gentle, and shy unless they get scared or mad.

I look at my notes again. Oh no! The first paragraph is supposed to be the introduction. I just outlined the second paragraph.

I draw another gorilla, then design a house that we could build for him on the playground—a jungle house with a thatched roof. Cool! Estella's dad is an architect. He shows me his sketches sometimes. Underneath I draw letters the way architects do:

ROGILA HOUSS

My brain bounces back to soccer practice. I've been working on my corner kicks. I hope I get to do some today.

I'd better get this outline done. Did I misspell any words? A lot of them don't look right. I take out a clean sheet of paper and start again. When I finish the first and second paragraphs, I look up at the clock. It's almost lunchtime! Which is good, because I'm starving. But after lunch we have social studies and science and then it's time to go home. Is this due today?

I look over at Jake. He's reading a book. He's done already? Estella's still writing, but I see other kids who are finished, too.

Ms. Anderson stands up. "All right, class," she says. "Please hand in your outline on the way to lunch. If it's not done, your homework is to finish it."

Desks squeak open and shut as kids put away their stuff before they leave for lunch.

"And one more thing before I excuse you," she adds. "Writing an essay is one of the most important skills that you learn in fourth grade. You'll be using it from now on. Your fifth grade teacher will expect you to know how to do it. At the end of next week, we'll be having an essay test. It's your chance to show what you know."

My stomach switches from starving to jittery. All tests make me nervous. But a five-paragraph essay test? Scary. Scarier than any other kind of test. Scarier than a gazillion spelling tests.

Chapter 2

Soccer Practice

Finally school is over. Nellie is waiting outside our classroom when Jake, Estella, and I come out.

"First soccer practice today!" I say, as I dribble an imaginary ball.

"Cool!" Jake hoists up his backpack. "Every Tuesday and Thursday now?"

"Yep! And games on Saturday." I watch a monarch butterfly drift across the schoolyard and land on a eucalyptus tree.

"Are you glad to be done with tutoring?" Estella swings around the lamppost as we wait at the crosswalk.

"Tutoring was okay." Ms. O'Dell, the crossing guard,

waves for us to follow her across the street. "But soccer's the best."

"Where's practice?" asks Nellie.

"Beach Street Park." I kick a pebble across the sidewalk.

Until now, I could only be on a soccer team during summer vacation. Tuesdays and Thursdays after school I went to Monarch Masters Tutoring Center. The tutors helped me learn to read and write better. I got passing grades in everything on my last report card. So, after I asked for the millionth time, Mom and Dad said I could take a break from tutoring and be on a regular soccer team. That made me so happy!

"Bye!" I say to Nellie, Jake, and Estella when we're in front of my house.

I jog to the front door, go in, and toss my backpack onto the couch. "Mom! I'm home!"

My sister Emma is at the kitchen table drawing. She's in second grade, so she gets home earlier than I do.

"Hi Adam!" she yells out to me. "Can you help me make a castle?"

I grab an apple from the bowl on the counter and look over Emma's shoulder. "Looks good, Emma," I say. "Now show that it's made of stones."

Emma hands me her pencil. I sketch part of a rectangle. "See?" I explain. "You don't have to fill in the whole thing, just give the idea."

"Thanks. I get it." Emma draws more stones.

"Where's Mom?" I ask.

The back door opens and Mom and Liam come in. Liam looks hot and sweaty. He's wearing my old soccer shinguards, even though they're too big for him. I got new ones last weekend.

"Hi Adam!" Liam sets the soccer ball down on the kitchen floor and gets ready to kick.

"Pick it up, Liam. That's for outside." Mom says.

"Hey, Liam." I pick up the ball myself and spin it on my finger. "How was kindergarten?"

"We learned vows today. A, E, I, O, U." Liam takes the ball back and tries to spin it but it falls and bounces onto the floor.

"Vowels?" I grab the ball and hand it back.

"Right, vows." Liam still talks funny. He's only five.

"Ready for soccer?" Mom gives me a kiss on the head.

"Can't wait!" I run to my room, change into shorts, and pull on my new shin guards.

"Looking good." Mom smiles when I come back. "Remember, straight to the park and then back here to do your homework."

"Yes, mom." I don't want to think about homework right now. I want to get to the park and see who else is on the team.

"Have fun!" Mom calls as I open the door.

"Bye." I swing the door shut and jog away.

As I round the corner I see four kids from my school, and four from Pacific Elementary. I recognize them from the summer team. A man in a white T-shirt and red hat is with them. That must be the coach.

"Hey," I say, dribbling my ball down the field.

Riley, Jessie, Antonio, and Ryan run alongside of me. We kick the ball back and forth.

"Over here, boys." The coach waves us back. "You must be Adam. Nice to have you on the team. I'm Coach Carlos, Antonio's dad." He holds out a hand and I give him a good handshake, like my dad taught me. He is actually my stepdad, but he has raised me, so I call him dad.

Antonio is in Nellie's class. He and his dad look alike: dark hair, brown eyes, round faces. "Nice to meet you, Coach Carlos," I say.

"We're going to start practice in just a minute," he replies. We're a new team, so we need to pick a name. Here's your homework. Come up with a team name. What does the name mean? Why is it right for us? On Thursday, bring your best idea. You can present it, and we'll vote on Saturday before the game. Now let's get to work."

We run onto the field and Coach watches us dribble. He gives us pointers on switching legs and making our feet point in the right direction. He splits us into two groups and we play Monkey in the Middle. A couple of times Coach says "Good work, Adam."

I can't believe it when he calls out, "That's it for today, team." We just started! Could it really be an hour-and-a-half later?

I run over to my teammates and we slap hands with each other before we leave the field.

As I jog home, I think of team names. Lots of teams have animal names—badgers, dolphins, bobcats. The name we pick will be on our T-shirts with a picture. What would be good?

I see Jake as I pass the community garden and say hi.

He tosses some weeds into the bin and hops over the low fence. "Hi, Adam." Jake is wearing his NASA T-shirt. Magnus, his neighbor's dog, puts his front paws on the fence and wags his tail.

"You helping Mrs. Jensen with her garden again? And her dog?" I ask.

"Yep," he says. "Now that I've got my robot race car, I'm saving up for a rocket kit. So I'm earning extra money for that. How was soccer?"

"Awesome!" I boom out. "Antonio's dad is coach. We have a good team. We have to think of a name for it."

Jake pushes his glasses up and makes a dirt mark on his nose. "Astronauts?" he suggests.

I think about it. "Maybe," I say. "Thanks for the idea." But it doesn't seem like the perfect name. I give Magnus a scratch behind the ears before I leave.

At home, Liam's building a LEGO fort, Emma's reading, and Mom's making dinner.

"How was it?" Mom calls out.

"So awesome!" I say as I run into the kitchen, sit on the floor, and take off my shoes and shinguards.

Mom smiles and says, "Good! I know how badly you want to be on a soccer team. I hope it works out."

I don't like the sound of that. Hope it works out? Why wouldn't it?

"You said you have homework?" Mom slides the carrots she'd been slicing into the salad.

"Oh, right," I say. I'd forgotten all about homework and the essay test. Now it hits me like a soccer ball in the stomach. Mom's talking about the deal I made with her and Dad. If I want to play soccer, I have to keep up with my schoolwork. And get passing grades. And now I have to pass the five-paragraph essay test. Yikes! Can I do it?

Chapter 3

The Rockets

Mom says she or Dad will help me with my homework after dinner, but I decide to try to do it on my own. That way I'll get it over with sooner and I can watch TV. Plus, Mom and Dad won't think I need tutoring again.

I put away my soccer stuff and take my homework to the kitchen desk. I pull out my papers from school and get to work.

First I use the computer to check the spelling on the words that look funny. Ms. Anderson says it's not cheating to do this. But she also says I have to keep learning to spell words on my own. I wonder if I can use a spell-checker during the test?

Mom is making biscuits. I smell chicken in the oven. Yum! I'm starving.

I find some words that are wrong and fix them. Then I add them to my computer Spelling Pal list. It's one of the things I learned about at tutoring. The Spelling Pal program has a game that I play to practice the words.

I can't stop thinking about soccer practice. It's so cool to finally be on a team! What team name should I take to practice on Thursday? I think about Jake's idea. Astronauts are cool, but I picture them floating around in their spacesuits. Slowly. Our team needs a fast name. How about Rockets? I make a sketch of a rocket blasting off. I like it! I add a cloud of smoke at the base and a loopy dotted line to show its path.

The door swings open and Dad comes in carrying a paper bag. "Smells good in here!" he says cheerfully. He gives Mom a kiss and sets the bag on the table.

"What's in there?" Emma says as she and Liam come into the kitchen. Liam climbs up on a chair and looks inside.

"I thought you kids would like to try out the new colored pencils," Dad says. He and Mom own Monarch Grove Art Supply on Beach Street. Dad runs the store, and Mom goes in to help out when we're at school. It's the coolest place. The local schools and the university buy their art stuff there.

Emma brings me a pack of pencils.

"Thanks, Dad," I say. I open the package and pick a red one for my rocket.

"How's it going?" Dad comes over and puts his hands on my shoulders. "Uh-oh. Are you doing homework or drawing rockets?"

"Almost done with my homework," I say, sliding my sketchbook under the outline.

"Good. Don't forget our deal." Dad gives me a rub on the head and goes to wash up for dinner.

Emma is still standing next to me, reading my outline. "You're getting a gorilla?" she asks, sounding amazed. I'm amazed that she can read that quickly.

For a second-grader, my sister is a whiz at reading. "I wish," I say. "It's a five-paragraph essay outline. I have to say which animal would make a good classroom pet, and why."

"Oh." Emma looks it over. "So you need three reasons why gorillas are good?"

"Exactly," I say. She is so smart she gets it right away.

"Why five paragraphs if you only need three reasons?" she asks.

"Because ..." What are the other two paragraphs? Now I can't remember! This essay thing is a nightmare!

"You wrote *rogilla*," Emma says, pointing to my page.

"Oops, you're right," I reply. "I didn't see that."

Mom sets the breadbasket on the table. "Time to eat."

"Will I have to write essays in fourth grade?" Emma sits down next to me.

"Yep," I say. "You have to know how to get to fifth grade." Just saying this makes my stomach squeeze.

I'm pretty sure that's what Ms. Anderson said: that if I don't pass the test, I won't go on to fifth grade.

"You've been working on essays for a while now." Mom passes me a plate. "All that practice will pay off, I'm sure."

"There's a test at the end of next week," I answer. "I'm nervous about it." I pull a warm biscuit out of the basket and butter it.

"Well, you still have a lot of time to study," says Dad.

"I know. I'm going to," I say. I hold my breath and wiggle my feet under the table, which makes my chair squeak. Is Dad going to say I have to skip soccer practice so I can study more?

"Well, don't forget our deal, Adam. Schoolwork comes first, soccer second. Right?" Dad says.

"Right," I reply. It's bad enough trying to pass the essay test. But now I'm thinking I might not get to stay on the soccer team. On top of this, I wonder why Dad is always so worried about how I'm doing in school. Is it because he thinks I can't keep up? Is he right?

Emma says, "Dad, want to see my family portrait? We had to draw one for the bulletin board at Open House."

"Sure," says Dad.

Emma runs into her room and comes back with her drawing. Our family is lined up from tall to short: Dad, Mom, Emma, Liam, and I are standing side by side. Everyone but me has brown, wavy hair, and dark brown eyes. There I am, right in the middle, with red hair, green eyes, and a million freckles. I look more like my first dad, I guess. Sometimes I wish he were here. Maybe he'd be less disappointed in me than this dad.

Chapter 4

Emergency Meeting

After dinner I sit down to finish my outline.

"Want some help, Adam?" Dad asks. Mom and Dad help me a lot with my schoolwork. When I first went to tutoring, one of them came, too. The tutors showed us different tricks and tools to help me study.

"I'm good," I say, though I know I should say I need help. When I get tired, which I am now, the letters and words jump around on the page. Then it's so much work to read that I feel like giving up. But I don't want Dad to see me having trouble. He might think I can't do it. And be disappointed in me.

Emma and Liam get their homework and sit at the kitchen table.

I read over what I've done so far. I think I fixed all the spelling. I used the computer spell-checker. But what about the test? I'm not going to have a computer.

A message pops up on the screen. It's an email from Nellie to me, Estella, and Jake. I click it open and read. *You want to come over after school tomorrow? Lucy and Amanda are trying new cupcake recipes and they want us to vote on the best one.*

Lucy and Amanda are Nellie and Jake's older sisters. They hope to be on *Cupcake Wars* some day. They're always practicing.

I write back. *Sure. Sounds good.*

Back to my outline. Why is this taking so long? I decide to set the timer for fifteen minutes. It's a trick I got from tutoring: work till the timer beeps and then take a break.

I go back to work. I need examples of gorillas being playful and smart. I draw pictures of gorillas in my sketchbook, to come up with ideas. For some reason this works better than words. My favorite is a gorilla playing soccer with me. I do an Internet search for *gorilla*.

This helps too, though I don't see any information on gorillas as pets. Still, I make it up as I go along. I'm more than halfway done when the timer sounds.

"How's it going?" Dad comes into the kitchen. "Time for a break? How was soccer?"

I show him my rocket drawing. "Wouldn't this look cool on our soccer T-shirts?" I ask.

"Nice!" he replies. "Rockets is a good name. They're fast and powerful."

"I'm done, Dad." Emma hands Dad her worksheet.

"Looks great, Emma." Dad hands it back and Emma puts it into her backpack.

"I'm done, too." Liam slides off his chair and brings over his list of words.

Dad looks it over. "Can you read all of them?"

"*Ant, pet, lip, pot, tub, face, me, kite, go, tube,*" Liam says.

"Way to go," Dad says.

He high-fives Liam and I wish it were me. I mean, when even a five-year-old is better with words than I am it makes me want to tackle someone with my pet gorilla.

"Can we watch TV?" Emma asks.

"One show," says Dad.

I sigh and watch Emma and Liam bounce into the living room. How much longer is this outline going to take?

"You're almost done," Dad says, giving me a pat on the back before he leaves. I hear Liam dump LEGOs onto the coffee table.

I set the timer and get back to work. I finish as the timer sounds, set my paper aside, and copy the rocket from my sketchbook onto a clean sheet of paper.

Mom comes in to make herself a cup of tea. "All done?"

"Yep!" I call out.

"Want me to read it over?" she asks.

"No, I think it's okay. I used the spell-checker," I say.

I'm tired of working on this, and if Mom finds

anything wrong, I'll have to do more. Mom picks up my rocket drawing and looks at it. "Did Coach Carlos ask for drawings, or just names for the team?"

"Just names," I say.

"You should show him your drawing too, Adam," she says. "This is really good."

"Okay, maybe," I reply. How cool would that be? To name the team and design the T-shirts!

I shade in the sides of the rocket to make it look like a cylinder.

"Do you feel ready for your test?" Mom pours water from the steaming kettle into her mug.

I shrug and say, "Sure. I think so." But here's what I'm really thinking. *My practice essays take me so long! I have to take them home to finish. What if I don't get done in time when we take the test? What if I misspell too many words?* But I don't want to say this to Mom or Dad.

Mom dunks her teabag up and down. "You could talk to Ms. Anderson. She might give you extra time, or let you use a computer," she says.

"I'll be okay," I reply. "I don't want to be treated differently from everyone else."

"Everybody's different," Mom says. "It's not a bad thing. Some kids couldn't draw a rocket like yours or play soccer as well as you do."

"I guess," I say, but I don't feel great.

"Would you like me to talk to Ms. Anderson with you?" Mom asks.

"Naw, I'll be okay," I say, though I'm not sure it's true.

"Well, at least think about it," Mom says.

Another message pops up on the computer. Jake writes, *I can come: no gardening tomorrow.* Then from Estella, *Cupcakes, yum! I'll be there.*

Then it hits me: of course! Why didn't I think of this sooner? I hit Reply All and type *Since we'll all be at Nellie's tomorrow after school, want to have a Worry Warriors Meeting? Agenda: Five-Paragraf Essay Test.*

Chapter 5

I-See-One-Two-Three

After school the next day we meet in Nellie's backyard clubhouse. That's where we always have our Worry Warriors meetings.

The clubhouse is really cool. Nellie's dad built it for Nellie's brother, Henry, when he was little. Henry started high school this year and he's on the track team, so he's pretty busy. He lets us use it anytime we want.

We put on the Viking helmets that we got at the "after Halloween" sale a couple of years ago. We know we're a bit old for this now, but it's tradition.

Then we raise our hands and yell, "Don't worry, be happy!" That's our Worry Warriors battle cry. It's how we always start meetings.

"I hereby call this meeting to order," says Nellie. "Today's worry is the Five-Paragraph Essay Test next week. My class is having one, too. So, let's start by saying what worries us about the test."

We settle into beanbag chairs.

"And remember," says Estella, "nobody is allowed to say someone's worry is stupid."

"Right," I say. "What happens in the clubhouse, stays in the clubhouse."

"No making fun or laughing," adds Jake.

I start. "I'm sort of getting the hang of it. But it takes me so long! What if I run out of time? Also, I always have to look at my notes to remind myself what the five paragraphs are."

Estella nods. "I have trouble getting it done fast too."

"I also worry that we're going to have to read a passage and then use it to write the essay," I say. "I do better if I can get the information from videos or audiobooks." That's another trick I learned at tutoring.

Nellie speaks up. "I wonder if we'll have a choice of topics? I do best on narrative."

Jake nods. "I'm better at expository."

Estella frowns. "I forget the difference."

"Me too!" I say. "I think Ms. Anderson said you don't get to go to fifth grade if you can't pass the test." My heart *ka-thunks* just thinking about this. I feel like the wrestling gorilla is winning. Maybe it's not such a good idea to have one as a pet?

"Is that true?" Estella jiggles her feet.

Jake and Nellie shrug and shake their heads. I guess they don't worry about making it to fifth grade.

"And here's a huge, gigantic worry for me," I add. "The only way I could get Mom and Dad to let me play soccer was to promise I'd get passing grades. If I don't, I have to quit the team and go back to tutoring."

Everyone looks at me with a serious face. They know how much I want to stay in soccer.

"It's time to make a plan," Nellie says.

She raises one arm in a Worry Warrior sign.

"You're not quitting soccer." Estella raises an arm.

"You're going to ace this test." Jake's arm goes up.

I smile and raise both arms. "Let's do it. What's the plan?"

"Don't you use little rhyming codes to help you remember stuff?" asks Nellie. "Like 'I before E except after C'? That kind of thing?"

"Good idea!" I say. "I can make one up to remember the order of the paragraphs. I wish I had my language arts notebook with me."

Nellie and Jake are like walking, talking language arts notebooks. "Introduction, three supporting paragraphs, conclusion," they say together.

"How about I-one-two-three-C?" I ask.

"I-See-One-Two-Three sounds better," says Jake.

"That works. I can remember the One-Two-Three goes in between the I-See. Cool!" I say.

"Let's practice," says Nellie. "We'll write a quick essay together. Who wants to pick a topic?"

"*What would you do if you found out you were heir to the throne?*" says Estella.

I laugh. "You've got to stop watching *The Princess Diaries*, Estella."

Nellie smiles. "*Why we should have more free-reading time at school.*"

I laugh again. "Seriously?"

Jake says, "*Who is your favorite astronaut? And why?*"

"The guy who walked on the moon—because he's the only one I know! But I can't remember his name," I say.

Jake shakes his head. "Okay, you pick the topic, Adam. What's something you know how to do in soccer?"

"Dribble?" I say.

"Good," Jake says. "So the topic is, *How to Dribble a Soccer Ball*. You start and we'll help. Use the whiteboard."

Jake's mom gave us a big whiteboard a while ago.

She's a math teacher, so she has stuff like that. Nellie's Dad hung it up for us. Now I grab a marker and start.

"Wait," says Nellie. "You forgot to brainstorm."

"Oh, right." I talk as I draw sketches on the board. "Use both feet. Kick lightly. Keep control. Touch the ball with the inside of your shoes. It's okay to use the outside too. Don't look down. Know which direction you're going. The more you practice, the faster you'll get."

"Wow, Adam." Nellie puts her hands on her hips and stares at the whiteboard. "You know a lot about this."

"You could be a coach," says Estella.

I look at my sketches. "But the next part is where I get stuck," I say. "I can tell you guys how to dribble, and draw pictures, but turning it into an essay gets confusing."

"Let's use Adam's ideas to come up with an outline," says Jake. "I'll time it so we can practice working quickly, and then we'll compare."

We grab pencils and Jake says, "Go."

I think about and number my page like an outline.

Then I start filling it in. I don't even worry about spelling for now. But when Jake says "Stop!" I'm only halfway done. Jake and Nellie are finished, and Estella is on her last paragraph.

I take a deep breath and drop my pencil. It's not looking good for fifth grade. Or the soccer team. Where are Lucy and Amanda? I could use a cupcake right about now.

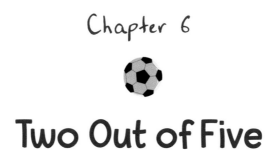

Two Out of Five

The next day at school I get more bad news.

The day before, Ms. Anderson had returned our class pet outlines. I thought I had fixed everything, but there were a lot of red marks for spelling:

Gorillas our the perfect classroom pit

Gorillas are easy too feet

Gorillas our playful

They lick to goof round

Then she told us to use the outlines and write the essay. I worked fast, finished it, and turned it in on time. I knew the spelling looked wrong on a few words, but I thought I did okay.

Today when she hands back the essays, I know I'm in trouble. I got a two out of five! Five is the best you can get, and zero is the worst. Three is a passing grade. Two is not. Mom and Dad are not going to like it.

"Some of you did quite well on your essay. Others need more practice. But you'll get it—don't give up."

Ms. Anderson hands a stack of papers to Estella and says, "Today we're going to practice a persuasive essay. Jessie, remind us of the purpose of a persuasive essay."

"Um, I don't remember. To entertain?" Jessie shrugs.

"What does persuade mean, Jessie?" Ms. Anderson waits for Jessie to answer.

"It means like, when you persuade your parents to give you more allowance?" Jessie says.

"Right! What's another word for persuade?" she asks.

"Talk them into it?" he asks.

Ms. Anderson nods and then says, "Exactly. Grace, will you read today's topic to the class, please?"

Grace reads: *Should all fourth graders play team sports? Why or why not?*

"First we're going to form groups," Ms. Anderson says."We'll talk together to come up with ideas. Then you'll work by yourselves to outline your essay." Ms. Anderson reads off the groups.

Estella, Grace, Riley, Jessie, and I slide our desks together.

"I say yes," Riley talks first. "Team sports are the best. I've been on a soccer team and a baseball league since I was little."

"Soccer is awesome," says Jessie. "Everyone should be on a team. I'm glad you got on our team, Adam."

"But not everybody wants to do team sports," says Estella. "I don't."

"You go to dance lessons," I say.

"I do too." Grace puts her arms out like a ballerina. "You have to be in time with the other dancers to look good. That's like a team sport."

"What about kids who don't do any of that?" says Riley. "Maybe they're not getting any exercise."

Ms. Anderson moves from group to group. "Write down notes as you talk. So you'll have your ideas ready when it's time to do your outline. Any questions? Need help?"

I think about asking Ms. Anderson if we can use the class computer to check our spelling during the test. But I don't want to make a big deal about it. Nobody else is asking, so I don't either.

"Adam, can I talk to you for a minute?" she says.

Uh-oh. This doesn't sound good. I follow her to her desk.

Luckily Ms. Anderson talks softly so the other kids can't hear. " I wanted to go over your last essay with you," she says. "You had some great ideas, and you remembered the five paragraphs. It was the misspelled words and the paragraphs that were out of order that brought your score down."

I look at the red marks on my paper. I can't believe I mispelled so many! *Rogilla* for gorilla, *pit* instead of pet, and *plaful* instead of playful. And, in the paragraph about what a gorilla likes to eat, I put examples of being smart.

"Do you have any questions?" she asks.

I decide to ask about spell-checking. "You said it's okay to use my computer to check the spelling at home. Can I do that on the test?" I say.

"Hmmm." Ms. Anderson rests her chin on her hand. "Normally it's okay to use a print dictionary."

I frown. Finding a word in a print dictionary takes me forever.

"But the librarian just got some handheld electronic spellcheckers. I'll see if I can get a few for the test," she says, when she looks at me and sees my worry.

"Thanks, Ms. Anderson," I say.

She smiles. "It's nice to see you working so hard, Adam."

I feel better. If Ms. Anderson is going to get a few spell-checkers, I won't be the only one in class who uses one.

Ms. Anderson tells us to go back to our own desks and write our outlines. I look at the clock, set an imaginary timer for fifteen minutes, and get right to work. I think for a minute. Should all fourth graders play team sports? I write:

All forth graders hoo want to play team sports shood get to. But if they dont want too, they cood do somethin else, like dancing or art. Thy should get exersise some way.

I resist saying they could exercise by playing with a pet gorilla. I know that's another essay altogether. But it does make me laugh.

I think my arguments are pretty good. But then, maybe they should have to try team sports even if they don't think they'd like it. And then maybe they would decide they like it. But if they don't like it, then they can choose something else. Can I figure out how to fit all this into my outline?

I get the introduction, first, and second paragraphs outlined before Ms. Anderson tells us it's time to stop. "Please turn in your outlines if they're done," she says. "Otherwise, finish them at home tonight and bring them back in the morning."

Homework on soccer practice day again! At least I got further this time than I did last time. And I feel like I know what I'm doing. And I get to use a spellchecker on the test. But, I'm definitely waiting until after soccer practice to show Mom and Dad my two out of five.

Chapter 7

Good Idea

I hurry home after school, change into my shorts, pull on my shin guards, grab my rocket drawing, and stuff it into my pocket before I go.

Riley, Jessie, and Antonio are already dribbling and I join in. When the other guys come, Coach sets up some orange cones and we practice weaving in and out around the cones. He shows us how to use the inside, outside, and bottoms of our shoes to tap the ball lightly and make it move in different directions.

"Nice work, Adam! Way to go, Riley!" Coach Carlos claps his hands together.

I tap the ball as I run and remember to keep my head up. It's a warm day. I'm breathing hard and feeling great.

"Over here, Adam!" Antonio says. I kick the ball to him and he moves it down the field. The other players and I run along with him and cheer when he kicks it into the goal.

Next we practice throwing. Coach shows us how to throw the ball up in the air, clap three times, and jump up in the air to catch it. Then we swing the ball behind our backs, throw it through our legs, do a forward roll, and get the ball before it gets too far away. It looks funny. I laugh so hard my stomach hurts.

After that, we split into two groups and play a practice game. We're pretty evenly matched, and when Coach Carlos signals us that practice is over, the score is tied. He waves his arm for us to come over. "That's it for today," he says. "Before we go, everyone sit down for a minute. Did you remember to bring ideas for a team name?"

I reach into my pocket for my paper and then raise my hand.

"What've you got, Adam?" he asks.

I hold up my drawing. "I think Rockets would be a cool name for our team," I say. "Rockets are fast and powerful."

"Wow, nice drawing!" Jessie and Riley say together.

"You drew that?" Antonio seems amazed.

"You spelled Rockets wrong," says Ryan.

I look at my paper. *ORKKETS*. It does look wrong! Why didn't I spell-check it?

Coach Carlos grins at me. "No worries. We can fix the spelling. Other ideas?"

"Sharks," says Jessie. "They're tough and scary."

"Rams," says Riley. "They're mean and big."

"Bulldozers," says Ryan. "They're fighting machines.

"Tornados," says Antonio. "They're destroyers."

The rest of the guys didn't bring ideas. We hand our papers to Coach Carlos and he tells us to think it over and we'll take a vote next time.

I'm starving when I get home. "What's for dinner?" I ask Mom when I find her in the kitchen.

"Tacos. What's for homework?"

"More essay stuff. I got my other essay back today."
I might as well get this over with. "I didn't do so well," I
say, "but Ms. Anderson helped me in class today. So, I don't
think it's anything to worry about."

Mom dries her hands and takes the paper from me.
"Two out of five? You need a three to pass, right?"

"It's just a practice essay," I say. "And now that I know
what I did wrong, I'll do better." I don't tell Mom that I'm
super-worried. Then she'll be worried, and Dad will be
worried, and they might make me go back to tutoring.
But what if I don't pass the real test?

Mom hands the paper back to me. "I know you're
working hard, Adam. And I know you love soccer. But
maybe you still need some help from the tutoring center."

Exactly what I was afraid of! "Really, Mom," I say.
"It's just a one-time thing. I'm going to work on my next
essay right now."

"Okay, but let's talk some more about it when Dad gets
home," she replies.

The back door swings open and Dad comes in. "Talk about what?" he asks.

"Hi, Dad. How was your day?" I reply. Maybe if I act like it's no big deal that I got a two, Dad won't think it's a big deal, either. I hide the paper behind my back.

"Good. What's that behind your back, son?" Dad gives me a rub on the head with one hand, and takes the essay from me with the other.

"It's just a practice essay," I say. "I didn't quite pass, but I talked to Ms. Anderson about it and she showed me how to fix it. I'm working on another one right now." I'm not sure if acting like I'm not worried is helping or hurting. Maybe Mom and Dad think I don't care about the test. I add, "I'm going to do better on my next practice. And on the test."

Dad takes my essay and starts to read.

"You don't need to read it," I say, hoping he'll stop reading. "It's just a dumb essay."

He looks at me and smiles, which I didn't expect.

"It's not dumb," he says, handing it back to me. "You make some good points."

I take a deep breath. Is Dad okay with my not-passing score?

"But we have a deal, right?" he adds. "You need to get passing grades in order to stay out of tutoring and on the soccer team."

"But, Dad—" I start to say, but he stops me.

"Hang on, Adam," he says. "I know this is a practice essay. And I know you're working hard on your school skills. So, this is a warning. You need to keep working. You've got another week before the test."

I let out a big breath. Whew! "Okay. I'll keep practicing. I promise," I say.

"Good job." Dad holds up a hand for a high-five. "Let's eat, I'm starving."

As soon as we're done with dinner I get to work. But it's hard to concentrate.

I keep thinking, *What if I don't pass the test and Dad and Mom say I can't stay on the soccer team?* I sketch soccer balls and rockets and test papers and electronic spell-checkers as I think. Suddenly an idea pops into my head. I draw a lightbulb with rays shooting out as I make a plan. It's good!

I click open the email program and type a quick message to Nellie, Jake, and Estella. *I need help with an idea. Worry Warriors meeting after skool tomorrow?*

Chapter 8

The Art of Persuasion

Friday after school we go to Nellie's for another Worry Warriors meeting.

"I got a two-out-of-five on my last essay," I tell Jake, Nellie, and Estella.

"Bummer." Jake says. "But it was just a practice essay."

"Can I see it?" Nellie holds out her hand for the paper.

"Did you tell your mom and dad?" asks Estella.

"Yes," I say. " That's why I called this meeting. "They say if I don't pass the test next week, I have to go back to tutoring. Which means no soccer team."

"No!" Jake, Estella, and Nellie say together.

I nod. "No passing score, no soccer team."

"That would be awful," Estella frowns.

"We'll help you practice." Nellie finishes reading my essay, says "Not bad!" and hands it to Jake.

"Even though you got a two, there were a lot of things you did right," says Jake. "I mean, you did spell *rogilla* a few times, but your ideas about letting them eat all the bugs in the grass is good. Even though you put them in the paragraph that was supposed to be about being smart."

"I know!" I say. "I do think I'm getting better at it. And Ms. Anderson says I can use a spell-checker on the test. But now I feel so worried about not passing, I'm afraid I'll mess up on the test just from being nervous. So, I have an idea."

"What is it?" ask Jake, Nellie, and Estella together.

"What if I write a persuasive essay to convince my dad and mom that they should let me be on the soccer team, even if I don't pass the test?" I suggest.

"How are you going to do that?" asks Nellie.

"I hope there's more to this plan," says Jake.

I grab a marker and write on the whiteboard. *Shood all forth grabers play team sports? Why or why not?*

"Our topic yesterday is what gave me the idea," I explain. "One thing they always told me at tutoring was that you have to focus on what you're good at." I draw a soccer ball whizzing across the whiteboard.

"You're awesome at soccer," says Nellie.

"And art," says Estella. "But wasn't the reason for tutoring to help you with what you're not good at?"

"Yes," I say. "But the tutors would set the timer for fifteen minutes of writing practice, and then I'd take a break and we'd kick the ball around for five minutes or I'd draw."

"I get it," says Jake. "You want to show your mom and dad that you'll do your schoolwork better if you get to play soccer too."

"Right!" I exclaim. "And that I'll be able to relax and study for the test if I know I'll still get to do soccer.

What do you think? Is it possible it would work?" I ask. I hold my breath while they think about it.

"I do!" Nellie smiles. "Tell how being good at one thing helps you do other stuff well."

"And your mom and dad will see that you can write a persuasive essay," Jake says.

"And that you're practicing," says Estella. "You could also write about how it's good for your health to get fresh air and exercise. Parents love that kind of stuff."

I start writing ideas on the whiteboard. Nellie, Jake, and Estella help me turn my ideas into an outline.

"You know what else would be good?" I say before I start my essay. "A list of people with dyslexia who are successful. At the tutoring center, they had a poster like that. I think it would be good to remind my dad."

"I bet we could find it on the Internet," says Jake.

"No wi-fi out here," says Nellie. "But I'll go use the computer in the kitchen. You guys keep working on the essay."

All this practice is making me faster. In just a little while, I finish writing. Estella reads my essay out loud. It sounds pretty good. Jakes helps me fix my spelling errors. Then Nellie comes back with a few printed pages.

"Wow, Adam!" she says. "I didn't know all these people had dyslexia. Look at this list." Nellie sits down at the table and we crowd around.

The printout has actors, artists, architects, athletes, business owners, filmmakers, inventors, scientists, judges, musicians, doctors, and even writers.

"Leonardo da Vinci?" asks Jake.

"And Daniel Radcliffe," says Nellie. "I love the Harry Potter books and movies."

"Stephen Spielberg!" Estella's eyes go wide. "I love *his* movies too."

"Thanks, Nellie," I say. "This is the list they had at tutoring. Can you believe it? Some of the people on this list didn't even know they had it. It's so cool that even though they had trouble reading, they did awesome stuff. Like art, or movies, or writing books. My tutors said maybe they were good at stuff *because* their brains work differently."

Nellie staples the list to the back of my essay. Before we end the meeting, we raise our arms in the air and do a Worry Warriors battle cry. "Don't worry! Be happy!"

I'll be happy if I pass the test and get to stay on the soccer team.

Chapter 9

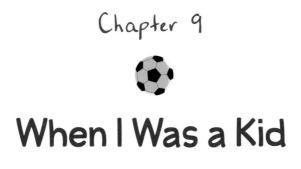

When I Was a Kid

When I get home from Nellie's, Mom says Dad has to work late tonight and all day tomorrow.

"So, he's not coming to my first soccer game?" I say. I really wanted Dad to see me play tomorrow."

"I'm sorry, Adam," Mom says. "You know he would if he could. But I'll be there, and Emma and Liam." Mom sets a bowl of pasta on the table.

I'm disappointed that Dad's not home. Now I'll have to wait until tomorrow night to see what he says about my essay.

In the morning, I'm ready for the soccer game right after breakfast. Mom says I should go ahead to the park and she and Emma and Liam will be there before the game starts.

I jog to the park and see most of the guys seated on the grass. The other team is on the far side of the field. The families of the teams are on blankets or in folding chairs along the edges of the field.

"Okay," Coach Carlos says. He holds a stack of papers in his hand. "Anyone else bring an idea for a team name? It's time to vote."

Nobody has a new name, so Coach reads off the names from last time. "Sharks, Rams, Bulldozers, Tornados," Coach holds up my drawing, "or Rockets?"

"I like Rockets," says Ryan.

"I do too," says Jessie. "I like Rockets better than Sharks, even though I thought of Sharks."

"Me too," says Riley. "I think Adam's drawing would look awesome on our T-shirts."

"Could we do that?" Antonio asks his dad. "Could we use Adam's drawing for our T-shirts?"

"Sure," says Coach Carlos. "If everyone votes for it."

I can't believe it when all the guys on the team raise their hands.

"We're the Rockets!" says Ryan.

"Blast-off!" says Antonio.

I smile and raise my arms into the air just as I see Mom, Emma, and Liam walk up. "Go Rockets!"

We didn't winn, but the game was still a lot of fun. As soon as it's over, I start thinking about our next practice.

After the game Mom takes us to the Beach Street Sandwich Shop for lunch, and then we get frozen yogurt.

The afternoon seems so long after that. I keep waiting to hear Dad come home. He doesn't usually work on Saturday. If he does, he comes home early. Today he doesn't get home until right before dinner. He looks tired, and he doesn't even ask about my soccer game.

When he comes back to the kitchen after washing up, I'm waiting at the table with my essay.

"What a day!" He sits down across from me. "The store was busy. I'm glad tomorrow's Sunday. "

I hand him my essay. "So Dad," I say. "I wrote a practice essay. For you and Mom."

Dad takes it and reads it over. He looks at the list of people who have dyslexia.

My heart pounds. Is he going to agree?

"This is a good essay, Adam." He looks up at me. "I'm curious. What made you give me this list?"

"Well," I shuffle my feet under the table. "I wasn't sure if you knew that, well, that people with dyslexia can be artists and doctors and architects and stuff."

"Adam." Dad looks serious. "Of course they can. *You* can. You can be anything you want."

"Really?" I say. "Because, I thought—I thought you were worried that I'm not going to be able to do stuff like other people. Since reading and writing are hard for me.

"And I'm not as smart as your other two kids," I add. "Your real kids."

Dad is quiet for a minute. "Did I ever tell you about when I was a kid? About baseball?"

"No," I say, curious to hear what he has to say.

"I must have been eleven, or maybe twelve," he says. "I liked school okay. I got good grades. I loved to draw, just as you do. I was always sketching. But I was awful at sports."

"You were?" I ask, surprised.

"Horrible. I was always the last one picked for gym," he says.

"Really?" I'm surprised.

"It didn't bother me too much because I didn't really like sports," Dad says. "I'd rather read or draw or make stuff in the woodshop. But in junior high, a lot of my friends tried out for the baseball team, and I decided I wanted to play."

"Did you try out?" I ask.

"I was going to," he says. "Some of my buddies helped me practice. But I just wasn't good at it. I worried that I'd try out and not make it. And be embarrassed. So, you know what I did?"

"What?" I ask.

"I gave up. I stopped practicing, and I didn't try out. It still bothers me to think about it," Dad says sadly.

"Wow," I say. I never thought about Dad giving up. Or not being good at something.

"So, do you know why I'm telling you this, Adam?" he asks.

I shake my head.

"Because you are so much like me," he says. "You couldn't be more my real kid if you tried. And I don't want you to ever give up. I know schoolwork is hard for you. But I also know you can do it as long as you keep trying."

I almost choke up with tears, but I manage not to even though Dad hugs me. I hang on tight till I get my act together. "Thanks, Dad," I say. "I thought you were worried

about my schoolwork because you think I'm not going to be able to do it."

"No way," he responds. "Exactly the opposite. I know you *can* do it. Just like all the people on your list. And I want you to have the chance to be anything you want to be."

"Oh." I think about this for a minute. This is really good news. I have a feeling my persuasive essay worked, too. Just to be sure, I ask, "Did my essay persuade you?"

Dad smiles and holds up his hand for a high-five. "It did. If Mom agrees, you can stay on the soccer team."

Chapter 10

Test Day

On Tuesday at soccer practice, Coach Carlos says our T-shirts will be ready on Thursday. I can't wait to see them!

We write a practice essay at school on Wednesday. Ms. Anderson sends me to get five handheld spell-checkers from the library. She shows the whole class how to use them, and says we can take one to our desk if we need to. I use one during my practice test, and so do some of the other kids.

On Thursday at soccer practice we get our T-shirts. They're gray, with a red rocket blasting off, and the word ROCKETS in yellow letters underneath. I feel like a real artist. The other kids slap me high-fives and say, "Way to

go, Adam." Coach says we should wear our T-shirts to the game on Saturday.

When I get home from practice, I try on my T-shirt for Mom and Emma and Liam. Mom takes a photo with her phone and we text it to Dad, Jake, Nellie, Estella, Grandma, and Grandpa.

On Friday morning, Jake, Nellie, Estella, and I talk about the test on our way to school.

"What are I-See-One-Two-Three?" Nellie quizzes us.

"Introduction and conclusion with three supporting paragraphs in between," Estella and I chant together.

"And the three types?" Jake walks backward in front of us.

"Narrative-Expository-Persuasive," Estella and I say.

"Yay!" Nellie and Jake give us a thumbs-up.

"What do you do before you outline?" Nellie asks.

"Brainstorm!" Estella and I know this. We're ready.

We give each other a Worry Warriors hand-tap before we round the corner to cross the street with Ms. O'Dell, the crossing guard.

In class, Ms. Anderson does the regular morning stuff—attendance, announcements, monitor jobs. Then she says it's time for the Five Paragraph Essay Test.

My heart bangs as Estella hands out the papers. Ms. Anderson says to go ahead and I read the topic.

I get right to work. When I'm done, I look at the clock and see I have time for spell-checking. I enter the words that look funny, fix them, and read my essay over one more time.

My Ideal Job

by Adam Brown

When I grow up, my ideal job wood be artist, architect, or soccer champ. I draw in my sketchdook every day. Sometimes I draw besigns for buildings. I'm also on a soccer teem. Artist, architect, or soccer champ are all good jobs for me because I no how to do them and I lick doing them.

I think I could be a good artist. My parents own an art supply store so I always have sketchbooks and pencils. I practice every bay, and draw things, like people, buildings, animals, superheroes, and cars. The rocket I drew got chosen to bee on the T-shift four my soccer team. Four all of these reasons, I think artist wood be a good jod for me.

Another job I'd like is architect. Estella's dad is an architect, and sometimes he shoes me his plans and we talk about how he draws them. An architect is a type of artist, which I alreaby talked about. And I like to build stuff with LEGOs, so that's good practice. Since I know an architect, and am good at art and building, I think architect would be a good job for me.

Or I could be a pro soccer player when I grow up. I can dribble fast without losing control of the ball, and I keep my head up so I don't run into anyone by accident. I don't get mad and say bad words if my team doesn't win, so I'm a good sport. I can play for a long time without even getting tired. Four all of these reasons I think I'd be a good soccer player.

I guess since I'm only nine, I can't see into the future and no if I'll bee an artist, an architect, or a soccer player. Right now I'm mostly trying to get from fourth to fifth grade. But one good thing I no is, that I won't ever give up on what I decide to be. I'll learn all about it and practice and make sure I'm good at it, even if it takes a long time.

I know it isn't perfect but I think it's good! I take a deep breath and turn my paper over to show Ms. Anderson I'm done.

Then I open my sketchbook and draw the Rockets, zooming down the soccer field together to score a goal.

ABOUT THE AUTHOR

Marne Ventura is the author of twenty-nine children's books, ten of them for Capstone. A former elementary school teacher, she holds a master's degree in education from the University of California. When she's not writing, she enjoys arts and crafts, cooking and baking, and spending time with her family. Marne lives with her husband on the central coast of California. This is her first venture into fiction.

ABOUT THE ILLUSTRATOR

Leo Trinidad is an illustrator and animator who has created many animated characters and television shows for companies including Disney and Dreamworks, but his great passion is illustrating children's books. Leo graduated with honors from the Veritas University of Arts and Design in San Jose, Costa Rica, where he lives with his wife and daughter. Visit him online at www.leotrinidad.com

GLOSSARY

architect—a person who designs buildings and advises in their construction

dyslexia—a learning disability that is usually marked by problems in reading, spelling, and writing

essay—a short piece of writing that tells a person's thoughts or opinions on a subjectoutl

eucalyptus—a fragrant evergreen tree that grows in dry climates

expository—writing that explains something

narrative—telling a story about something that happened

outline—a written list of the most important parts of an essay

persuasion—trying to change someone's mind

Viking—a group of Scandinavian warriors who raided Europe in the 8th to 10th centuries

whiteboard—a large board with a smooth white surface that can be written on with special markers

TALK ABOUT IT

1. Adam was really worried that he'd flunk the test but he wouldn't share his worries with his mom and dad. Do you think he should have? Why or why not?

2. Adam doesn't want extra help, even though he's entitled to it as someone with dyslexia. Do you think the extra help would have made him feel better or worse? Explain your reasoning.

3. If you had to choose a classroom pet, what would it be? Why?

WRITE ABOUT IT

1. Think about a time you wanted something really badly but your parents didn't agree. Write a persuasive essay to see if you can change their minds.

2. Using the five-paragraph essay technique, write about an interesting adventure you had during the summer.

3. How might you have helped Adam with his worry? Write a step-by-step account of the practical things you might do to help.